DATE DUE		
DEC 15 2005		OCT 02 2010
SEP 14 2010		
JAN 11 2011		JUN 30 2013

Robin Hood in the Greenwood

Other books by Jane Louise Curry

(*Margaret K. McElderry Books*)

ROBIN HOOD
in the Greenwood

retold by
JANE LOUISE CURRY

illustrated by
JULIE DOWNING

Margaret K. McElderry Books

Margaret K. McElderry Books
An imprint of Simon & Schuster Children's Publishing Division
1230 Avenue of the Americas
New York, New York 10020

The text of this book is set in Bembo.
The illustrations were rendered in pencil.
Printed in the United States of America

First Edition
10 9 8 7 6 5 4 3 2 1
Library of Congress Cataloging-in-Publication Data
Curry, Jane Louise.
Robin Hood in the greenwood / retold by Jane Louise Curry ;
illustrated by Julie Downing. — 1st ed.
p.   cm.
Summary: Recounts further adventures of Robin Hood, the English hero who lived as an outlaw with
his followers in Sherwood Forest and dedicated his life to fighting tyranny.
ISBN 0-689-80147-5
1. Robin Hood (Legendary character) — Legends. [1. Robin Hood (Legendary character)—Legends.
2. Folklore—England.] I. Downing, Julie, ill.
II. Robin Hood (Legend). English. III. Title.
PZ8.1.C97Roi   1995
398.2'0942'02—dc20   95-4447
                                                                                        CIP
                                                                                        AC

Retold from the fifteenth-century poem "A Lytell Geste of Robyn Hode"
and early ballads.

For Paul
—J. L. C.

Contents

ROBIN HOOD AND THE ARCHER FRIAR

Summer was the best of times in Sherwood Forest. In summer, Robin Hood's outlaws ate as well as kings do. Hunting was easy. Deer roamed the forest. Farmers nearby had the fruits of field and orchard to sell. The miller sold fine flour. And the outlaws shared all they gathered with the homeless folk who lived in the forest.

The outlaws of Sherwood were no ordinary robbers. Robin Hood's rules were strict. Women could pass through the forest freely. So could honest men who earned livings by the work of their own hands.

Not all travelers were safe. Robin had no love for officials and merchants and churchmen. They often cheated the poor of their pennies and the unlucky of their land. The outlaws made such men join them for dinner in Sherwood, then took all of their money.

Other rich travelers also left with their purses half empty. Their wagons and packhorses left with lighter loads too.

When no travelers rode the forest roads, Robin's men spent the day in sport. Some ran foot races. Some shot at targets with their bows and arrows. Some wrestled, and others played at fighting with quarterstaffs.

One day Robin spied three of his men, small Much, big Little John, and tall Will Scarlet, who only sat and told tales.

"Ho, you sacks of lazy bones!" he said. "Are you such good archers that you need no practice? Come, bring your bows and show me what you can do."

Robin led the way through the wood. Soon they saw a small herd of red deer far ahead. Much put an arrow to his bow and let fly. Three hundred feet away a fat buck fell. Will Scarlet loosed his shaft next. It flew four hundred feet to bring down a doe.

Little John scoffed. "That is nothing!" He aimed and sent an arrow a hundred feet further still. A huge hart with wide antlers fell dead.

"Oho!" Robin cried. "Tonight we eat well! I would ride a hundred miles to find another who shoots as well as Little John."

Will Scarlet laughed. "Why ride so far? Fountains Abbey is nearer. A friar lives there who will beat even you. Set your archers all in a row and he will outshoot them every one."

"A friar?" Robin frowned. "Friars do not live in abbeys. Only monks do."

"This friar does," said Will. "Once he wandered the kingdom to preach God's word. Then he marched with the king's army to the Holy Land. Now he thinks a warm bed and good food better than blistered feet. At the abbey he tends the abbot's dogs instead of souls."

"I like the sound of him," Robin said. "Indeed, I shall not eat a bite or drink a sip until we meet!"

So Robin dressed himself in ragged clothes. He fastened a broadsword and buckler onto his belt. He slung his bow and sheaf of arrows over his shoulder. Then he mounted the oldest horse in the outlaw camp. As he rode out of the forest, he looked like a soldier just home from the wars.

"This we must see!" Will Scarlet said. So he and all the others followed.

In Fountaindale, Robin came to a wide stream. The old horse would not cross it.

Not far off, a man in a long friar's robe came walking along the riverbank. A broadsword and buckler hung at his side.

Robin saw a chance to make mischief. He tied his horse to a thorn tree. Then he strode to the water's side and stood in the friar's way. "You have a broad back, Brother," he said. "Carry me across the stream."

Without a word the friar took Robin on his back. Without a word he waded through the waist-deep water.

On the far side, Robin leaped down. "My thanks, good friar."

The friar scowled. "If you wish to thank me, carry me back over the water," he growled.

Robin had an angry gleam in his eye. He had not expected this, but he took the friar upon his back. He splashed into the water and soon was back on the side from which he started. The friar leaped down and set off once more along the path.

"Hold, pesky friar!" Robin shouted. He ran to put himself in the friar's way. "Carry me over the stream again. If you do not, I will beat your backside black and blue."

Without a word the friar took Robin back upon his back. He waded into the water waist-deep. When

he came to the middle, he threw Robin in with a great splash.

"Sink or swim, you lazy lout!" he roared. "I care not which."

Robin splashed his way to the bank. Dripping and angry, he put an arrow to his bow, and shot. The friar raised his buckler and knocked the arrow aside.

Robin shot again and again until his last arrow was gone. Each time the friar knocked the arrow out of the air. Robin drew his sword, but the friar was ready for him.

Their swords and bucklers clashed and clanged. They crashed and bashed, and battered and banged. Neither could get the better of the other. At last they had to stop to catch their breath.

"Friar," Robin said as soon as he could speak. "A favor, I beg you. Allow me to blow three notes on my horn."

"Blow away," the friar grumbled. "Blow till your eyes fall out, for all I care."

So Robin Hood raised his horn and blew three blasts. At once half a hundred outlaws came running from the woods. Robin folded his arms and laughed.

The friar scowled. "Then I must beg a favor too. Let me put my fist to my mouth and whoo three whoos."

"Whoo on," said Robin. "I like nothing better than to hear a friar whoo."

So the friar set his fist to his mouth and whooed three long, loud *whoooo-oos.* At once half a hundred huge hunting dogs came running down the dale. The friar drew his sword again.

"Here's a hound for every man," he roared at Robin, "and I myself for you."

"Wait!" Robin held up his hand. "You must be the man I seek. I was wrong to lose my temper— *Ai!*" He cried out as two dogs dashed up and tore at his cloak.

Little John raised his bow. "Call off your hounds, friar!"

"Who are you to order me, fellow?" the friar bellowed.

"I am Little John, Robin Hood's man. Call off your dogs or I will skewer them and you."

"Robin Hood?" The friar dropped his sword. "Put up your bow, good John. Call me Brother Tuck. I am no enemy to Robin Hood."

"Then prove yourself my friend," Robin said. "Come with us to Sherwood. You are too good a fighter to be a kennel keeper. Teach us what you know of sword and bow. Preach to us each Sunday.

We will give you a gold noble for every sermon, and a new robe each holiday."

"*And* as much good meat as you can eat," Little John put in.

"With as much ale as you can drink," Much added.

Friar Tuck gave a loud laugh. "Hah! Why did you not say so sooner? I will fetch my bow and be in Sherwood by suppertime!"

And he was.

ROBIN HOOD AND THE PLUCKY PAGE

One summer day a farmer from Barnesdale brought sad news to Sherwood. Robin's father had died in May, and his mother in June.

When Robin heard this, he dressed himself in a friar's robe and set out for Gamwell Hall. His uncle, Sir George Gamwell, lived halfway between Robin's old home in Barnesdale and Sherwood Forest.

Sir George told the unhappy tale. "The sheriff of Nottingham came with fifteen men-at-arms. He took your father's farm. 'A thief and traitor's family should not own barns and cattle and good rich land,' he said. 'They will go to the king's true friends.'"

Robin's heart grew hot with anger. "The king never had a friend more true than my father."

Sir George sighed. "Alas, it broke your father's

heart. His death broke your mother's. Others have lost their farms too. When good Sir John of Barneswell died, the sheriff claimed his lands for the king."

"What of Sir John's daughter, my old playmate Marian? Surely the lands are hers."

Sir George shook his head. "She has gone to the king's court in London. Now that she is alone in the world, the king is her guardian. He will choose a husband for her."

When he heard this, Robin's heart was heavy. As a boy he had loved Sir John's little daughter. Marian, when she was small, had sworn to marry Robin or no one at all.

"Some day the sheriff will pay," he promised.

Back in Sherwood, Robin called his men together. "Take word to every yeoman in the county," he said. "If any man needs tax money to save his land, he can send to Robin Hood for help."

Robin himself went to tell the miller at Newstead. He dressed as a friar and left Sherwood by a secret path.

He returned the same way. Halfway home he

heard a rustle of leaves and the sound of footsteps nearby. Robin drew his sword from under his robe and stepped behind a tree.

From his hiding place he saw a stranger, a boy, hurrying his way. The boy was dressed like a page who serves a rich knight. His boots were made of fine leather, his suit of rich cloth. He wore a sword at his belt, and a fat purse too.

Robin Hood stepped into the path.

"Ho, boy! Hold where you are!"

The boy answered bravely. "Why should I? This is the king's forest, and I am a king's man."

"Are you, indeed?" Robin laughed and bowed low. "Unless you are the king himself, you must pay a toll. Rich folk who wish to walk in Sherwood must pay. We have many mouths to feed. Give me half of what you carry in that purse, and you may wander where you please."

"No!" The page put his hand on the hilt of his sword. "You are dressed like a friar, but friars do not talk of tolls. Friars do not wear swords. Take care! I carry a friend at my side." He drew his blade.

"You are a bold puppy," said Robin. "I shall have to teach you a lesson with the flat of my blade on your backside."

"You may try," the page said. He made a slash with his sword in the air.

Robin laughed and knocked the blow aside. He did not laugh for long. The page was small and his reach was short, but he was brave. He was quick of eye, and faster of foot.

Before long, Robin was huffing and puffing. His sleeve was slashed and his sword hand gashed. The page's arm was cut, and his face was pale. Still he fought on.

"Hold your hand, boy!" Robin cried. "My band of good fellows needs brave lads like you. Come live a free life in the greenwood with Robin Hood." He pushed back his hood and held out his hand.

"Robin?" For a moment the page stood as still as a stone. Then he laughed and pulled back his own hood. Down spilled long locks of red-brown hair.

The page was not a boy at all, but a young woman. She ran to give Robin a happy kiss. "I have found you at last!"

"Marian!" Robin could scarcely believe his eyes. "Here, and not in London? How?" He gave her a hearty hug.

Maid Marian smiled. "It is a long tale."

"Come, then," Robin said. "Come have your hurts bound up, dear love. Tell me as we go."

So as they went, Marian told her tale. When the sheriff ordered that she must go to London, she made her plan. She would not let the king choose a stranger for her husband. She packed her father's sword and a page's clothing with her cloaks and gowns.

Her chance came soon. On the first night of the journey, the sheriff and his servants stopped at an inn not far from Sherwood.

"In the middle of the night I dressed in these clothes. I climbed down from my window. Then I ran to the forest.

"So here I am," she finished.

Robin kissed her for joy.

When Robin and Marian reached Robin's camp, the outlaws cheered to hear her tale. They set to work at once. Some built a shady bower and decked it with flowers. Others set up tables and benches. They brought great platters of meats and fruits, and bowls of nuts and flagons of wine.

When all was ready, Robin Hood sounded his

horn. All the folk of the forest came, old and young, poor folk and outlaws.

First, Friar Tuck blessed Robin and Marian. Then he blessed the food, and the feast began. The forest folk ate and drank and sang, and sang and drank and ate from noon until the moon and stars came out.

And the next day they feasted all over again.

THE GOLDEN ARROW

The sheriff of Nottingham and his men searched everywhere for Lady Marian. They rode up and down the highway and the side roads round about. They combed the fields and hedges. They did not look in Sherwood, for what lady would go where men feared to walk?

After three days the sheriff returned to Nottingham. The next day a wine merchant from Bristol came to him to complain. "Twenty rascals stopped me on the forest road," he said. "Nay, *fifty* men, and a pretty maid. They took a wagon and six barrels of wine!"

The sheriff stared. A maiden? Lady Marian? In Sherwood? With Robin Hood? He glared and his face grew red.

"The king shall hear of this!" he shouted. He

ordered his servants to pack for a journey. "Saddle the horses! I go to London to ask his help."

In London the king frowned as he listened. "You are the sheriff. Do your job. If you cannot find these fellows in the forest, use some trick to lure them out."

On his way home the sheriff pondered the king's advice. "How many men live in Sherwood?" he wondered. "Thirty? Forty? What trick will catch them all?" At last he had the perfect answer: a shooting contest.

The sheriff laughed aloud. "If the prize for the best shot is a rich one, every outlaw in Sherwood will come!"

In Nottingham, the sheriff sent for the best goldsmith in the town.

"Make me an arrow," he said. "Give it a shaft of silver colored with gold. Make the head pure gold, and the feathers too."

News of the contest and of the golden arrow flew from town to village, to farm and forest.

"The best archers in the kingdom will come!"

"He who shoots best will win an arrow of gold!"

"All the North Country will be there!"

When the news reached Sherwood, Robin Hood shouted, "Oho! The men of Sherwood will show them what shooting should be."

David of Doncaster stepped forward. "It is not safe, Master Robin. In town men whisper that the contest is a trap. They say the sheriff has set it to catch us."

Robin laughed. "All the better! We will snag the sheriff in his own snare."

"I am with Robin," Little John boomed. "Let us give the sheriff's tail a sharp twist. But we cannot go as ourselves. Our hoods and cloaks of Lincoln green will give us away."

"Little John is right," Robin said. "We have cloth for new cloaks, and tailors to stitch them."

The outlaws set to work. From their storehouse they wheeled out a wagon full of cloth. Two men who had been tailors cut hoods of all shapes, and cloaks of all sizes. With Maid Marian's help, the outlaws sewed seams and stitched hems.

On the day of the contest the outlaws put on tunics and hose of brown or gray. Their hoods and mantles were bright and bold. Robin chose a scarlet hood. Will Scarlet chose grass-green. Maid Marian wore plum-red and Little John blue. When Robin blew his horn a hundred merry archers gathered at the edge of the forest.

"We will go by twos and threes," Robin said. He and Maid Marian and Little John set off first down the road.

In Nottingham they joined the crowds at the castle field. Eight hundred archers were there to try for the golden arrow. Four times eight hundred people came to watch. Men dressed as farmers and foresters moved among them. Under their hoods they wore steel caps. They carried swords or crossbows.

"Sheriff's men," Robin whispered in Little John's ear. "No more than six of us will shoot at a time. The others must stay close and look out for danger."

A strip of sand marked the line where the archers would stand. Halfway down the field twenty targets stood in a row. David of Doncaster and Much were the first of the twenty to shoot. They missed the eye of the target by only a hair's width. Will Scarlet struck it full center.

Then Robin Hood shot. His shaft flew so true that it split Will's arrow in two. The crowd gave a great *Hurrah!*

Little John's shot hit the bull's-eye easily. Gilbert

White-Hand's arrow split Little John's, and the crowd shouted again. Only the sheriff did not cheer.

"Where are the outlaws?" he growled to his sergeant. "I do not see even one."

Turn by turn, all eight hundred men shot. Fifty scored in the target's eye. Then the targets were moved further down the field. Once again, Robin and Gilbert split the arrows that hit the bull's-eyes before their own.

"A wonder!" the Lord Mayor cried. "Not Robin Hood and the best of his men could shoot better than these lads."

Robin smiled to hear him say so.

"True." The sheriff grumbled. "I was sure that Robin Hood would come. It seems he is too timid to travel to town."

Robin heard, and the words stung. To himself he said, "You will know before long, Sir Sheriff, that Robin Hood was here."

Soon the fifty best archers were twenty. Then the twenty were five, and the five, two. Robin Hood was one of the two. The distance was greater than ever. The other man's arrow touched the rim of the target's eye. Robin hit it dead center, and won.

The Lord Mayor stepped forward. He carried the prize. "What is your name, good fellow?" he asked.

"Herbert of Huntley, Your Worship." Robin bowed low as he took the golden arrow. "I thank Your Worship."

The outlaws began to slip away by twos and threes. When Robin turned to follow, he did not get far. A fat, angry merchant caught at his cloak.

"Herbert of Huntley? Hah! If your name is

Herbert, it is Herbert of Sherwood. I saw you there. You helped steal my best silks!" He pulled back Robin's hood and raised a loud shout.

"Robin Hood! I have caught Robin Hood!" he cried.

The Outlaws Find
an Old Friend

Robin broke free and ran. The folk shouted.
Horns rang out.

"Shoot!" the sheriff shouted, but his men could
not. The crowd was too thick.

Robin raced along the road after his men. The
sheriff's officers followed. When a hundred outlaw
arrows came flying at them, they turned tail and ran
back to town.

"Huzzah!" the outlaws cheered.

"They will be back," Robin warned. "Where is
Little John?"

They found their friend under a tree, an arrow in
his knee.

"Leave me, Master," Little John said. "I cannot walk."

"God forbid!" cried little Much. "I will carry
you myself."

But Much was much too small. Two by two the outlaws took turns in propping Little John between them. He hopped and hobbled as fast as he could go.

Before long, the sheriff's men were back. Foresters came with them, and soldiers, and the sheriff himself. The outlaws stopped and shot their arrows, then ran, then stopped again.

"Sherwood Forest is too far," Robin shouted. "Try for the wood ahead!"

Two miles into the wood, they came to a great clearing. In its middle stood a castle. Robin strode to the edge of the moat. He called to the guard at the gate.

"Who is master of this house?"

A merry voice answered from a window above. "Sir Richard of Lee. And a good welcome to you, Robin Hood!"

The outlaws cheered to see the knight. Twice he had been their guest in Sherwood.

"What brings you to me?" asked Sir Richard.

"The sheriff and his men are at our heels," Robin shouted.

"Let down the drawbridge! Open the gates!" Sir Richard called to his servants. When the last outlaw was in, they closed the gates. They pulled up the drawbridge. The knight set his guards to watch from the walls.

"You were kind when I was poor and in need," Sir Richard told Robin. "Now my lady and I can repay you."

He ordered tables set up and tablecloths spread. Roast meats appeared, and rich sauces. There were fresh fruits and white bread, cakes and ale, spiced sweets and sweet wine.

"Sit you down, good friends," said Sir Richard. "When the sheriff comes, he must wait while we make merry!"

The sheriff of Nottingham stopped his men at the edge of the woods. The castle shutters were shut. Laughter and cheers and song floated out from the castle courtyard.

"He has taken the outlaws in!" the sheriff cried. He called up to the guards on the walls. "Ho, you! Tell the knight of Lee that the sheriff of Nottingham orders him to open his gate."

The gatekeeper opened the shutters of his window above the gate. "When he has eaten his dinner, you may tell him yourself," he called. Then he shut up his shutters again.

For an hour the sheriff rode up and down in a rage. At last Sir Richard came to the castle wall.

"Traitor knight!" the angry sheriff shouted. "You protect the king's enemies."

The knight answered proudly. "Sir Sheriff, I am the king's true knight. He is my lord. You are not. I will wait to hear what he himself has to say."

To Sir Richard's surprise, the sheriff's scowl became a smile. "I agree. The king shall decide," the sheriff said. He turned at once and rode away. As soon as he and his men were safely out of sight in the woods, he stopped them.

"Stay here to keep watch," he said. "Sir Richard will send a message to the king. Arrest the messenger. I shall ride to London to tell the king my own tale."

THE RESCUE OF SIR RICHARD

In two days the sheriff came to the king's great house at London. "Well, Sir Sheriff," the king said. "Why do you come so soon again?"

"First the wild robber Robin Hood stole away the Lady Marian," the sheriff lied. "Now he has joined the knight of Lee in a wicked plot. With the outlaws' help, Sir Richard plans to rule all the North Country."

The king stood up with an angry roar. "Then he is a knight no more. And he shall learn that *I* am king! In two weeks I will come to Nottingham. My men will carry Richard of Lee and Robin Hood to London in chains. Ride home swiftly, Sir Sheriff. You must hire a hundred archers to join us." To pay the archers, he gave the sheriff a fat purse of gold.

★   ★   ★

When the sheriff reached Nottingham, he sent for his spies. They told him that Robin Hood and his men had gone home to Sherwood.

The next day, the sheriff hired the hundred archers. Then he decided not to wait for the king.

"I must capture Sir Richard of Lee and hang him," he told himself. "He knows of the tax money I have kept and the farms I have stolen. He must tell the king no tales. Then I can ask for his lands as my reward."

So the sheriff went to arrest the knight of Lee. He and his men hid in the forest beyond the castle fields. They waited and watched for days. At last, one morning Sir Richard rode out to go hawking. With his hawk on his arm, he rode out to hunt rabbits.

The sheriff's men rushed from the wood. They caught Sir Richard at the river's edge. The sheriff almost danced for joy.

"I would rather hang Robin Hood than you," he told the knight. "But if I cannot hang the fox, a dog will do.

"Tie him to his horse hand and foot," the sheriff ordered. And he led the way back to Nottingham.

*   *   *

Sir Richard's wife, the Lady of Lee, had watched from a high castle window. She saw the trap sprung.

"Saddle my palfrey!" she called to the servants. She ran down the stairs. At the gate she watched until the last sheriff's man was out of sight. Then she rode north at a gallop. Deep in Sherwood Forest she found the outlaws.

"God save you all," she cried. "Master Robin, I come to beg a boon. Do not let them harm my husband! They bound him hand and foot to his horse and led him away."

"Who has taken him?" asked Robin. "And when and where?"

"Who but the proud sheriff?" the Lady of Lee answered. "Toward Nottingham. No more than an hour ago."

Robin blew three long notes on his horn and then three more. A hundred and forty men came hurrying.

"Belt on your swords and shoulder your bows!" Robin shouted. "We go to Nottingham to free Sir Richard of Lee."

Not a man stayed behind. With a shout, the outlaws raced toward town. Where the road bent, they went straight. They leaped hedges and ditches. They ran across fields and through woods. Lame Little John followed, riding the palfrey of the Lady of Lee, who waited in Sherwood with Maid Marian.

When the outlaws came to Nottingham they went straight in at the gate. The town folk scattered when they saw them. The outlaws, their faces fierce, filled the street from side to side.

As they came near the castle, they saw the sheriff and his men in the street ahead. Sir Richard was with them.

"Hold where you are, proud sheriff!" called Robin. "I wish to have a word with you."

"A word? I have two words for you," the sheriff shouted. He turned to his men-at-arms. "Shoot them! Shoot them every one!"

The officers fired their crossbows. The men of Sherwood shot too. The two flights of arrows passed in the air. Men cried out. More arrows flew. The sheriff fell with Robin's shaft in his shoulder.

"Lie there, false sheriff," Robin cried. "And bad luck to you, for no man alive can trust you."

At Robin's signal, the outlaws drew their swords. They rushed at their foes. Some of the sheriff's men

fought. Many fled. They sped to the castle gate and shut themselves safely in.

Robin ran to cut the ropes that bound Sir Richard to his saddle. "Stay by me," Robin said. He gave Sir Richard a bow and arrows.

"Now, Sir Knight, be ready to run for your life. One day the king will learn who are the true thieves, and who are the king's true men. Until then, you and your lady must stay with us in the greenwood."

Robin and his men hurried out of the town. They ran north over mire, moss, and field, and came at last to the safety of Sherwood.

THE KING RIDES NORTH

Fifty knights rode to Nottingham with the king. Their armor shone and their banners flew as they trotted into town. Everyone turned out to cheer them. Only the sheriff was not there. He was in bed, nursing his wounds.

The next day the king and his knights and foresters set out. From Nottingham they rode to Southwell and Bolsover. The following day they rode to Bakewell and Derby. They heard no news of Robin Hood, only that he must be "somewhere in Sherwood." But Sherwood was miles wide and deep. They crossed it by road and saw no one.

"In the past I have hunted deer across all this county," the king said. "Once there were many herds. Now there are few. Today we have seen only one hart with a good head of antlers."

"It is Robin Hood's doing," the chief forester said.

The king glared in anger. "I wish to see this Robber Hood face to face! Find him!" He galloped on.

The next day when the king's company made ready to ride out, the forester who stood beside the king's horse spoke softly.

"My lord king, if you wish to see good Robin Hood face to face, you may. There is a way."

"And what is that, pray?" the king asked.

"You must leave these knights and bowmen behind. Keep the packhorses and five of your best knights with you. There is an abbey nearby. Go borrow clothing from the monks there. Then I will lead you into Sherwood Forest. I swear to you, Robin Hood will come to rob us."

"Oho!" The king gave a loud laugh. "Disguises and danger! And if Robin Hood takes us to his camp, we will know where to find it again." So he chose his five best knights. The rest he sent back to Nottingham.

At the abbey the king borrowed a long gray robe and a wide gray hat from the abbot. The monks brought gray robes to the knights and the forester. Then seven newly made monks rode out toward the

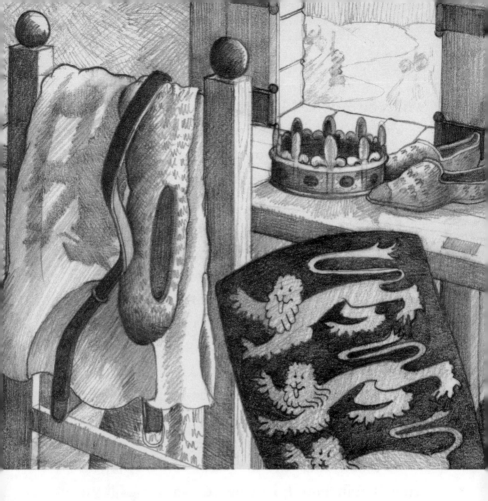

forest road. The king went first, and sang *Deo gratias* all the way to Sherwood.

They rode only a mile into the greenwood before they were stopped. Suddenly Robin Hood and a dozen of his merry men stood before them in the road.

Robin took the king's horse by its bridle. "Stay a

while, Sir Abbot. My name is Robin Hood. We are yeomen of this forest, who have only the king's deer to live on. You have your abbey and the rich lands you rent out. You must have gold a-plenty. For charity, give us a bit of it."

"Alas," the king said. "I have been with the king at Nottingham much of this week. We have spent most of our money to feed his knights and lords. I have only these forty pounds left. Yet truly, if I had a hundred, I would give it all to you."

"Fairly said," answered Robin. He took the forty pounds and divided it in half. Half he gave to his men, and half he returned to the king with a bow.

"Sir Abbot, keep this half. Perhaps we will meet another day, when you are richer."

"I thank you," the king replied. "But if you are truly Robin Hood, I bring you greetings from the king. He bids you come to Nottingham to meet him." And he showed Robin the king's great seal on a piece of parchment. When Robin saw it, he pulled off his hood and knelt in the dusty road.

"I love no man in all the world as well as I love our king," he said. "Sir Abbot, for the news you bring, today you shall dine with us."

"We thank you," the king answered. He looked at

his knights, and they at him. "What sort of robbers are these?" they all wondered.

Robin Hood led the king's horse to the camp by the outlaws' meeting tree. Fires blazed in the fire pits there, and venison was roasting on the spits.

Robin took down a great horn that hung on the tree trunk and blew as loud a note as he could blow. At once, a hundred and forty men came running.

"By Saint Austin!" the king said to himself. "His men obey him faster than mine do me."

When everyone sat down to the meal, Robin and Little John served the king. There were platters of roast venison and good white bread. There were pitchers of red wine and brown ale.

"Eat hearty," Robin said. "Afterward we shall give you a taste of the life we lead, so that you may tell the king."

When they rose from the table, the outlaws took up their bows. At first the king and his knights were alarmed. Then they saw men set up two targets.

"Ho! I love a good contest," the king said. "But you have set the marks fifty paces too far."

"Wait and see," Robin said. "The game is this: every archer who misses must pay me an arrow and take a good thump of my fist."

Some men hit the mark, and some won thumps. When all had shot, Robin took his turn. Alas! He missed by three fingers' width and more.

The outlaws laughed and gave a cheer. "Pay up, Master," said Gilbert. "And take your reward!"

"Fair enough," said Robin. "Sir Abbot, I give up my arrow to you. I pray you, pay me my prize."

"No, no," the king said. "It would not be right for a monk to hit a yeoman. I might hurt you."

"No fear." Robin laughed. "Hit away, as hard as you can."

So the king rolled up his sleeve. He gave Robin such a hearty thump that he fell flat onto the ground.

Robin gasped as he rose. "Sir Abbot, there is iron in your arm. Can you shoot as well as you—" He stopped and stared.

The abbot's hat had slipped off. For the first time, Robin and Sir Richard saw him full in the face. Both fell to their knees. Amazed, the other outlaws knelt too.

"My lord king of England!" Sir Richard exclaimed.

"God save us!" cried Robin. "My lord king, of your goodness have mercy on my good men and me. God save us, have mercy!"

"For God's sake I will," said the king. "But only if you and these good fellows will leave the greenwood and serve me. You must leave your robbers' life and come to live at my court in London."

Robin stood. "Indeed," he said, "I will. I vow to you and to God that I and my men will come— all hundred and forty and four of us."

Then he laughed. "But if we do not care for the life there, we will come home again, to hunt your dun deer."

Robin Hood and the King

"Tell me this, friend Robin," the king commanded. "Do you have any green cloth I may buy?"

Robin blinked in surprise. "Yes, sire. Forty yards and more."

"Good!" The king laughed. "Sell me enough for seven cloaks and seven hoods. Then find me fingers to sew them."

Robin gave orders, and in an hour the new garments were ready. The king pulled off his friar's robe and put on Lincoln green. His five knights and the forester cast off their gray robes too, and dressed in green.

"Now," the king said, "we shall ride together to Nottingham."

And so they did. One hundred and fifty-one men, the knight and Lady of Lee, and Maid Marian rode out of the forest to the Nottingham road. The poor folk whom the outlaws had sheltered and fed for so long followed them to the forest's edge. They waved a sad farewell.

The men made merry as they rode. Friar Tuck sang. Some of the outlaws told the knights tales of their adventures. The time passed so merrily that before they knew it, they had come in sight of Nottingham.

Women washing clothes in the river looked up. Guards on the city wall looked down. Ladies at the castle windows looked out. They saw the road full of fluttering green cloaks, and cried out.

"The robbers are coming!"

"Our king has been killed!"

"Robin Hood is coming to kill us all!"

In the town, the sheriff cowered in his bed. Men dashed in all directions. Children scattered and housewives wailed. Old women hurried home as fast as they could hobble.

The king laughed heartily to see them all flee. "They take me for an outlaw!" But then he took pity on them for their fright.

"Come out, good folk!" he shouted. "Come greet your king! From today, Robin Hood and his merry men are king's men. There are no outlaws left in Sherwood."

Everyone who heard marveled, "Can this be true?"

When they saw that the leader of the men in Lincoln green truly was their king, they were full of joy. To celebrate, they set out a great feast in the market square. There was food and drink for all, and singing and speeches.

At the end of the day, the king rose and gave back to Sir Richard of Lee his knighthood and his lands.

"Be the loyal knight that you were," the king said with a smile. "But take more care to keep the law!"

Robin Hood lived twelve months at the king's court in London, and then three more. At first the king kept Robin with him every day. He listened to Robin's tales and nodded. "Indeed, I must help the poor," he said. But day after week after month he did nothing.

Robin gave dinners for the lords and knights and

squires. They listened to his tales too. "Indeed, we should help the poor," they agreed. But they did nothing either. When Robin had no money left to feast them, they forgot him.

Robin's men did not care for town life. One by one they went out on errands and never came back. Only Marian and Little John and Will Scarlet stayed.

One day they four went to watch a shooting match in the king's park. Robin sighed to see the young men shoot.

"Once I was a good bowman, brave and strong," he said. "Folk named me the best archer in merry England. Alas, if I live any longer in the king's house, I will die of misery!"

So Robin went to kneel before the king.

"My lord king, grant what I ask. For seven nights I have not slept. For seven days I have not eaten. I am unhappy away from Sherwood. To be there again, I would willingly walk backward and barefoot all the way."

"Then," the king said, "if you must see Sherwood, you must. But see that you stay no more than seven days and seven nights."

"With all my heart I thank you, sire," Robin said.

It was a merry morning when Robin and Marian, Little John and Will rode into Sherwood. They smiled to hear the birds' songs and the rustle of the breeze through the trees. In a clearing ahead, deer grazed in the long grass.

"We have been away too long," Robin said. "I itch to shoot a good dun deer for our dinner."

Robin shot as true as ever. His first arrow brought down a handsome hart. His heart was so light that he lifted his horn and blew a loud note.

Little John laughed. "If any of our band are at hand, they will know who is here."

They were, and they did. One dropped at once from a tree. In minutes, many more came. Before long, every one of the old outlaw band was there. They pulled off their hoods and knelt.

"Welcome home to the greenwood, Master Robin!"

Robin threw his town hat in the air for joy. He never put it on again. He loved the king and feared to disobey him, but he would not return to London Town.

★　★　★

And so it was that Robin Hood stayed with his friends in the greenwood—hunting and eating and singing, robbing the rich and helping the poor—not for seven days and seven nights, but for twenty years and two.

SOME WORDS

An **abbey** is a place where a large group of **monks** live together like brothers. They have a church, a dormitory, a small hospital, gardens, and barns and farms.

An **abbot** is the churchman in charge of running an **abbey**.

A **buckler** was a small round shield a soldier used to protect himself from his enemy's sword.

Dun is a dull brown color.

A **friar** belongs to a brotherhood—an "order"—of churchmen. Many friars were preachers. Most made a promise to God to stay poor, since riches can make people selfish. Many begged for their food as they walked from town to town, preaching and doing good deeds.

A **hart** is a male red deer. Red deer live in Europe and Asia. They are related to North American elks, but are not as large.

A **moat** is a deep, wide trench around a castle. It was usually filled with water, so that enemies could not get near the castle walls. The bridge over a moat is a **drawbridge,** which could be pulled up at night, or when enemies attacked.

A **monk** is a man who decides to live apart from the bustle and violence of the world and closer to God. He lives with other monks in a monastery or **abbey.** He spends his time in work and prayer.

A **noble** was an English gold coin worth half of a **pound**, which is the name of the most important unit of money in England. In Robin Hood's time a pound was worth more than twenty present-day U.S. dollars.

A **page** was a boy who served a king or queen, lord or lady, knight, or other important person. Often the page's parents were important people themselves, and the page was being trained in manners and getting along in the grown-up world. He might have a number of different jobs, from carrying messages to serving his master at the dinner table.

A **palfrey** was a smallhorse with a smooth walk and trot. Ladies rode palfreys because, with their long skirts, they had to ride on sidesaddles, with both legs on the same side of the horse. A smooth ride made that much easier!

A **quarterstaff** was a strong wooden staff about as tall as a man, or a little taller. For fighting, it was held with one hand in the middle and the other hand between the middle and one end.

Venison is the name for deer meat.

A **yeoman** was a farmer who owned and worked his own land, or was the son of such a farmer.